dick bruna

miffy
at
school

SIMON AND SCHUSTER
London   New York   Sydney   Toronto   New Delhi

It's early in the morning.

Off to school the children go.

Miffy's in the red dress.

She's the one we know.

The journey doesn't take them long

on their little feet.

Their school looks very cosy

in its building nice and neat.

Their teacher's there to greet them

and check them in again.

She wears a lovely pendant

hanging on a chain.

The bell is rung for school to start.

The children all go in.

Once she sees them sitting down

the teacher can begin.

First we'll draw some loops, says Miss.

Let's keep them neat and tight.

We'll need these loops to form our letters

as we learn to write.

Let's have a go at adding up

these mushrooms that I drew.

Two mushrooms and three mushrooms –

what does that come to?

And now it's time to learn a song,

so every child stands.

Miss keeps their voices all in time,

conducting with her hands.

Then Miss pulls out some building blocks

for them to build a city.

With houses, church and gateway

doesn't it look pretty?

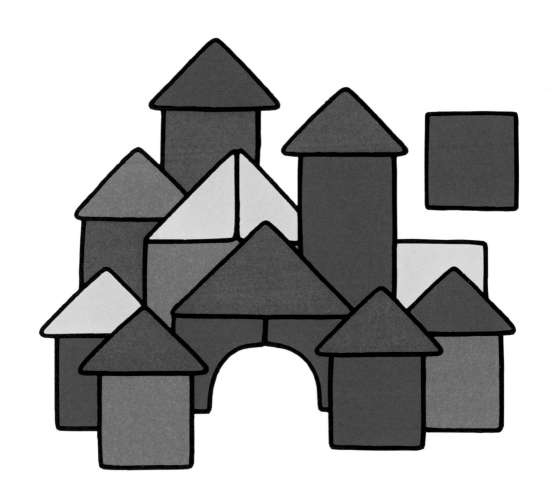

And after that it's playtime.

They play out on the grass.

They also do a little dance

to help the time to pass.

And now we'll draw, Miss tells them.

Miffy's very keen.

She draws a tree, a sun of blue,

and makes a pretty scene.

Miss puts up the drawings.

There really are a lot –

a castle, boats, a plane, a tree,

a house, a garden plot ...

Then Miss says, now it's story time.

She sits them on the floor.

Hooray! they cry, for story books

are something they adore!

Their story ends as home time

is rung out by the bell.

Miss waves them off while calling out

to wish their families well.

original title: nijntje op school
Original text Dick Bruna © copyright Mercis Publishing bv, 1984
Illustrations Dick Bruna © copyright Mercis bv, 1984
This edition published in Great Britain in 2014 by Simon and Schuster UK Limited,
1st Floor, 222 Gray's Inn Road, London WC1X 8HB
Publication licensed by Mercis Publishing bv, Amsterdam
English translation by Tony Mitton, 2014
ISBN 978-1-4711-2083-1
Printed and bound in China

www.simonandschuster.co.uk